JIG, FIG  AND MRS PIG

Written by PETER HANSARD

Illustrated by FRANCESCA MARTIN

WALKER BOOKS
AND SUBSIDIARIES
LONDON · BOSTON · SYDNEY

In a big old house on the far side of the bridge lived Mrs Pig, her son Fig and their servant Jig. If Mrs Pig was sour and cross all day, it was simply because that was her way. Mrs Pig was mingy, stingy and mean. And Fig, like his mother, was spoilt, bad-tempered and an awful pain.

Of course, Mrs Pig loved her son Fig because he was so very like herself.

"He's the apple of my eye," Mrs Pig would say fondly. "He's my Figsy-pigsy darling."

But if little Jig was cold, tired, hungry, or bullied by nasty Fig, Mrs Pig hardly even noticed.

For Astrid

P.H.

For Derek

F.M.

First published 1995
by Walker Books Ltd
87 Vauxhall Walk, London SE11 5HJ

2 4 6 8 10 9 7 5 3 1

This book has been typeset in Trump Medieval.

Printed in Italy

British Library Cataloguing in Publication Data
A catalogue record for this book is
available from the British Library.

ISBN 0-7445-3294-9

One of Jig's most difficult tasks was fetching the milk. Every single morning, rain or shine, Jig had to carry two heavy wooden pails all the way to town and back again.

All the same, despite day after day of endless drudgery, Jig would take up the pails and, in her sweet, clear voice, sing merry little songs so that she might forget that her load was heavy and the way was long.

One day, when returning home with the milk, Jig met an old pig.

"Please, may I take a sip from your pail?" asked the old pig. "I am very poor and very tired."

"Oh, of course you may," said Jig, even though she knew that Mrs Pig would be very angry and give her no lunch. "Please have as much as you want."

"You are ever so kind," said the old pig. "You shall have your reward."

With a sudden flash and a sudden crash and in a shimmer of golden light, the poor old pig changed into a wizard.

The wizard waved his magic wand once, waved his wand twice, and waved his wand thrice.

"Higgledy-piggledy, jiggery-spoke! I shall give you this gift: along with every word you speak, there will fall from your mouth a nugget of gold or a precious diamond."

Then with another flash and another crash, the wizard was gone.

When Jig got home, she found herself in big trouble.

"Some of my milk is missing!" shouted Mrs Pig. "You careless, stupid thing. There will be no lunch for you today and no dinner either."

"Quite right," said Fig, sticking out his tongue. "Fancy spilling our milk. What a silly piggy she is!"

"I'm ever so sorry," said Jig as two gleaming nuggets and two brilliant diamonds popped out of her mouth.

Mrs Pig snatched them up at once. "Where did you get these?" she demanded angrily.

Mrs Pig and Fig looked at Jig in astonishment as Jig told them all about the wizard. When she had finished, a glittering heap of gold and diamonds lay on the kitchen floor.

Next day, Mrs Pig told Fig to go to town for the milk instead of Jig.

"Surely you don't expect me to carry those heavy pails?" moaned Fig.

"I most certainly do!" said Mrs Pig firmly. "Go at once and keep an eye out for that old pig. I want gold! I want diamonds! And I want them now!"

Moaning and groaning, Fig took up the pails and set off for the town.

On the way home, Fig met a rich
young pig.

"I say," said the rich young pig,
"will you spare me a drop to drink?"

"No, I won't!" snapped nasty Fig.
"I haven't lugged this rotten milk all
the way from town just to waste it on
the likes of you. Push off!"

"You are not at all nice," said
the rich young pig. "You shall have
your reward."

With a sudden flash and a sudden crash and a shimmer of golden light, the rich young pig changed into a wizard.

The wizard waved his wand once, waved his wand twice, and waved his wand thrice.

"Higgledy-piggledy, figgery-joke! I shall give you this gift: along with every word you speak, there shall fall from your mouth a warty toad or a slithery snake."

Then with another flash and another crash, the wizard was gone.

"Speak to me!" said Mrs Pig, when Fig arrived home. "Speak to me, my Figsy-pigsy darling."

"I haven't got any gold or diamonds," cried Fig, spraying his mother with toads and snakes. "But it's not my fault! If Jig hadn't given our milk to that old pig in the first place, this would not have happened!"

Mrs Pig screamed in horror. "I hate toads and I can't stand snakes! Get away from me, you horrible, nasty, nasty thing!"

Pushing Fig aside, Mrs Pig ran squealing from the house. But no matter how fast she ran, nasty Fig stayed right behind her, clinging desperately to her apron strings.

Jig stood and watched as Mrs Pig and Fig, in a great clamour of squeals, shrieks, screams and grunts, raced away into the distance.

Then, after they had quite disappeared from view, she turned and went back inside.

"Oh, it's lovely having the house to myself," said little Jig. She put eight jewels in her pocket and sang this song:

"The sight of gold and diamonds
Gives everyone a thrill;
Yet kindly words and actions
Can be more precious still."

And so, as time went by, Jig became happier and richer. Of course, she did sometimes wonder if Mrs Pig and nasty Fig would ever come back, but as it happens... They never, never did.